FIRE UP WITH READING!

TONI BUZZEO

ILLUSTRATIONS BY SACHIKO YOSHIKAWA

Fort Atkinson, Wisconsin
www.upstartbooks.com

To Michelle, with deep appreciation
and many happy memories of our partnership.
—T. B.

To Shoji Nakasu.
Also, special thanks to Namiko Rudi.
—S. Y.

Published by UpstartBooks
W5527 State Road 106
P.O. Box 800
Fort Atkinson, Wisconsin 53538-0800
1-800-448-4887

Text © 2007 by Toni Buzzeo
Illustrations © 2007 by Sachiko Yoshikawa

On the first day of school, a dragon danced down the center aisle of the Liberty School auditorium.

I noticed fire engine tights. I spotted a dragon ring on the left pinky.

"Good grief, Patty Lee!" Carmen Rosa Peña poked me hard. "Who is THAT?"

"It's Mrs. Skorupski," I whispered. "You can tell by her accessories."

Our librarian climbed the stairs to the stage.
Her dragon head bobbled. Her dragon head sparkled.
It looked a lot like the head of the Chinese New Year
dragon dancing through the streets of my old Chinatown home.

She handed our principal, Mr. Moriarty, a rolled-up scroll.

"Hear ye! Hear ye!" He unfurled the scroll. "Commencing this day,
September 2, Liberty School shall fire up with reading."

Mrs. Skorupski struck a huge brass gong. I shivered as the deep sound
rang through the auditorium.

"I hereby challenge you," Mr. Moriarty continued, "to READ!"

Carmen sat up straighter. Kids around us whispered. The gong chimed again.

"All reading shall be measured in minutes," Mr. Moriarty read. "Futhermore, the teacher of the Top Reading Class shall be declared the Dragon-headed Teacher. He or she shall wear the dragon head in our Read Across America Day parade on March 2—precisely six months from today."

My new teacher, Mr. Dickinson, caught my eye and winked. I ducked behind my hair.

Carmen jumped out of her seat and chanted, "Mr. Dickinson! Mr. Dickinson!"

Mr. Moriarty cleared his throat. "The Top Reader in each grade shall also march in the dragon costume."

My head swirled. The dragon costume!

"Wooo-wooo-wooo!" Carmen pumped her fist.

Why did *she* have to be a fourth grader too?

Each dragon scale represents 30 minutes of reading. The first class to paste up all 5,000 scales will have fire-breathing status!

When we walked down the hallway, huge green paper dragons filled the wall space between the classrooms.

"Hey, Mr. Dickinson, look at this!" Carmen pointed to a large fishbowl of shiny paper dragon scales. On the bowl it read:

**Each dragon scale represents
30 minutes of reading.**

**The first class to paste up all 5,000
scales will have fire-breathing status!**

"We can do it, Fourth Graders!" Mr. Dickinson said.

Instantly, I was dreaming about dancing the dragon dance right behind Mr. Dickinson.

"Forget it, Patty," Carmen poked her elbow into my side then announced to the class, "*I'll* be the Top Fourth Grade Reader!"

"We'll just wait and see, Carmen," Mr. Dickinson said.

By the end of the day, Liberty School was all fired up about reading. The janitors and bus drivers were reading. The cafeteria ladies and crossing guards were reading. The kids and teachers were reading. All because of Mrs. Skorupski!

That first week, she helped me to discover new books and authors and to uncover old favorites. And she introduced me to entire library shelves I'd never explored before.

"Okily dokily," she said. "Go to it!"

From then on, every day felt like a reading holiday. I clocked at least two hours a day: over my oatmeal, while I brushed, during DEAR time and, of course, listening to Mr. Dickinson's read-aloud.

I wanted to read even more, but my mom said, "Exercise is as important as reading." So I rode my bike or rollerbladed after school while Carmen read. She was gluing on twice as many dragon scales as I was. I needed a plan.

"Patty Lee!" Tiny silver disks dangled from Mrs. Skorupski's ears. "I was hoping the Fourth Grade Reading Queen would visit the library today. What's up?"

"Carmen's reading minutes are up—again." I said.

"She's sure a reading fiend this year," Mrs. Skorupski said. "I'm proud of her."

Proud of Carmen? What about me? I glanced up at the poster she'd hung last week.

Listened to a good book lately?

I pointed at the poster. "Does listening to audiobooks count?"

"For Top Reader? Of course!" said Mrs. Skorupski. "Audio minutes count. Braille minutes count. All reading minutes count. Here, take two."

Audiobooks were a great plan!
During November, I read five
fabulous books—while I biked,
while I skated, even while I took a
bath.

By winter vacation, our class had
been Top Reading Class for four
months in a row, and I was 267
minutes ahead of Carmen Rosa
Peña at last. I left for the break
determined to keep my lead.

On the first day back to school, we stickered our dragon with the last of the fishbowl scales.

"Fire-breathers, you did it!" Mr. Dickinson shouted. "Patty, run down to the library and tell Mrs. Skorupski our dragon needs fire."

"Okily dokily!" Mrs. Skorupski's flame earrings dangled above the yards of yellow, red, and orange cellophane she carried down the hall.

That day, Mrs. Skorupski announced our fire-breathing status on the intercom and the monthly Top Readers by grade. I held my breath when she got to fourth grade.

"Carmen Rosa Peña."

Wait! What about my audiobook plan?

Carmen pulled an mp3 player from her backpack. "Audio downloads from the public library. Mrs. Skorupski told me about it."

I groaned.

Later, I stopped in to the library. "I'm desperate," I said. Then I described my new plan to Mrs. Skorupski.

"I'll think on it," she said.

On Friday morning, Mrs. Skorupski sent me a note:

Your presence is requested in the library!

Mrs. Skorupski

She waved me over to meet Mrs. Miller, a Kindergarten teacher.

Mrs. Skorupski's helping-hands earrings swayed. "Allow me to introduce Patty Lee."

Mrs. Miller shook my hand. "Raymond Woo really wants to be the kindergartener in that dragon costume," she said. "But he doesn't have anyone to read to him at home."

"Oh!" I said. "He's my neighbor. Maybe I could read to him."

"Wonderful," Mrs. Skorupski and Mrs. Miller said in unison.

You can always count on Mrs. Skorupski to help you with a plan.

After that, I read to Raymond every day during activity period. Then, I started visiting Raymond and his grandmother at home after dinner. By the end of January, I had pasted up twice as many scales as Carmen. And I helped Raymond paste his scales on his Kindergarten class dragon, too.

When Mrs. Skorupski announced my name as the Top Fourth Grade Reader for January, Carmen glared at me.

The next day, she wasn't in the cafeteria at lunch.

She wasn't jumping Double Dutch at recess.

She wasn't even on the bus ride home. My mom told me not to worry, so I walked next door to read to Raymond with his shiny smile and dragon costume dreams.

February 29, Leap Day, was the last day of Fire Up with Reading. Mr. Dickinson let us read all day. I spent both my recess and activity period reading Chinese New Year books with photos of dragon costumes to Raymond.

On March 1, I ran all the way to school and into the auditorium.

Mrs. Skorupski, holding the dragon head, made the final announcements.

"The Top Reading Class is Mr. Dickinson's Fourth Grade!"

Mr. Dickinson hopped up on his chair, and we cheered around him. Silence fell.

"Grade Five, a tie! Cindy Lord and Terry Farish."

I slipped out of my shoes so I could cross my toes.

"Grade Four."

I crossed my eyes, too.

"By only ninety minutes ..."

I held my breath.

"... Carmen Rosa Peña."

I gasped.

Carmen grinned at me and whispered, "Reading to the ELLs ... thanks for the idea."

I turned away and pulled my hood up over my head. I nearly missed hearing the Kindergarten winner.

"... Raymond Woo," Mrs. Skorupski said.

"You did it!" Mr. Dickinson shouted. Everyone turned to me.

I burst into tears.

Be a
Library
✦ ✦
Success
story ✦

Mrs. Skorupski sent a note down
after lunch:

Your Library Media Specialist
needs you!
Mrs. Skorupski

I dragged down the hallway. Mrs. Skorupski, wearing dragon-head earrings,
squatted next to Raymond.

"He won't walk in the dragon costume," Mrs. Skorupski said.

"But Raymond," I said. "That's why you wanted to be Top Reader."

Raymond shook his head. "Too scared," he whispered.

"What if I walk with you?" I glanced over at Mrs. Skorupski.

Raymond jumped up, slipped his hand in mine, and did a little skip.

"Okily dokily," said Mrs. Skorupski.

At 8:30 a.m. on March 2, television cameras lined the front walk.

Mr. Dickinson wore the dragon head. Carmen was stuck in the middle. Raymond and I wagged the tail.

At the front door, Mr. Moriarty banged the gong.

Mrs. Skorupski led us through the neighborhood three times, wearing her fire engine tights, dragon ring, and dragon-head earrings.

"I love to read!" Raymond shouted inside the dragon.

"Me, too!" I shouted back.

Then we finished the dragon dance parade,
all fired up with reading.